PASSAGE TO FORTUNE

Searching for Saguenay

Copyright © 2017 Stone Arch Books

All rights reserved. No part of this publication may be reproduced in whole or in part, or stored in a retrieval system, or transmitted in any form or by any means, electronic, mechanical, photocopying, recording, or otherwise, without written permission of the publisher.

Library of Congress Cataloging-in-Publication Data
Library of Congress Cataloging-in-Publication data is available on the Library of Congress website.
ISBN 978-1-4965-3481-1 (library binding)
ISBN 978-1-4965-3482-8 (paperback)
ISBN 978-1-4965-3483-5 (eBook PDF)

Editor: Brenda Haugen
Designer: Ted Williams
Cover Illustration: Rory Kurtz

Printed in China.
003259

CONNECT

PASSAGE TO FORTUNE

Searching for Saguenay

BY JESSICA GUNDERSON

STONE ARCH BOOKS
a capstone imprint

265
300
NW
10
20
30
40
50

Three Ships

You may have heard of me. I'm Samuel de la Loire, the youngest explorer of the New World. And the richest man on Earth.

You might wonder how I, just a kid, came to be the youngest and richest explorer the world has ever known.

Let me tell you my story from the beginning.

I was born into a wealthy aristocratic family in St. Malo, France. I had everything a thirteen-year-old kid could wish for — cooks to make my meals, a maid to make my bed, a private tutor to give me daily lessons. I had a father who groomed me to inherit his estate and take his place in the French Court. I had a good life.

But it wasn't what I wanted.

I wanted adventure. I wanted fame. I wanted fortune. My *own* fortune, not my father's.

I despised my daily lessons. And I hated the food the cooks made.

I was bored by the letters and numbers my tutor, Pierre St. Clair, made me practice. I often stared out the window at the clouds whisking quickly by, while Monsieur Pierre threw up his hands and cried, "Attention, Monsieur de la Loire! Pay attention!"

The words in the books St. Clair gave me blurred together until they resembled waves on the choppy sea. I leapt from my little desk, crossed my legs, and hopped up and down. "Monsieur St. Clair," I whined, "I must use the latrine."

He fell for it every time. He sighed. "Fine. Be back in five minutes, and we will go over your history lesson."

Of course I didn't really have to use the latrine. I scurried down the back staircase, dodging maids with armloads of laundry or pails of soapy water, and darted out the door into the bright sun.

I was free.

I knew exactly where I was going. The docks of St. Malo, where ships glided in and out of the harbor, manned by strong sailors who were weathered from sun and wind.

My boots slapped against the dock. In my tailored clothes, I was out of place here among the rough dockworkers. I nearly stumbled into one worker as he heaved a crate onto the dock. "Look out, fancy boy," he snarled.

Some of the dockworkers, though, waved and nodded. They were used to seeing me, my fancy clothes and all. "Morning, Sammy!" one called. I waved back, trying not to cringe at the nickname. *Sammy* made me sound so young. I preferred *Sam*. A strong sailor's name.

But anything was better than Monsieur de la Loire.

I stood at the edge of the dock, staring out at the harbor and breathing in the salty air. In the distance I spotted the dark silhouette of a ship. *Where was it going?* I wondered. *Where had it been?*

I knew it was only a matter of time before my tutor, Pierre, found me. And sure enough, he soon came bounding along the waterfront, his hair askew and his nose turned up at the smells of fish and saltwater.

"Monsieur de la Loire!" he called, panting.

I heard a sailor behind me snort with laughter. No one was called Monsieur here.

Pierre came to a stop beside me. He frantically wiped his sleeves, as though they were soiled and disease-ridden. "You are not allowed to go running off!" he said. A dockworker shouldered past him, knocking him off balance. His arms flailed, and he grasped my shoulder, eyes wide with fright. If I hadn't steadied him, he might have toppled face-first into the grimy harbor water.

Pierre swallowed, trying to remain calm, his eyes darting toward the murky water and back at me. "We must return to the estate at once. At once!" he cried.

I shrugged off his grip, took another deep breath, and sighed. I couldn't argue or refuse. If I did, he would fetch my father. And I certainly didn't want my father showing up on the docks.

Pierre took a trembling step away from the edge of the dock, glancing over his shoulder with alarm to make sure I was following him. I sighed once more and darted in front of him. "Follow *me*," I told him as I marched easily through the throngs of peddlers, fishermen, and sailors.

I decided to take the long way home. Pierre wouldn't notice, or even if he did, he would follow meekly. He knew I could have my father fire him in an instant, and he'd end up jobless like the beggars on the docks.

We reached the southern tip of the harbor, and I was about to lead Pierre down a dark alley path when a sight stopped me. Three tall ships moored, silent and regal. No activity bustled around them. These ships weren't normal cargo ships. No, these were special.

The *Grande Hermine*, the *Petite Hermine*, and the *Emerillon*.

The names stuck with me as we trekked back to the estate.

I didn't know then that these three ships would change my life.

265
300
NW

THE DINNER GUEST

Days passed in their normal, boring fashion. I longed to return to the harbor and catch a second glimpse of the three moored ships. I longed to taste the saltwater on my tongue and feel the sea winds on my face.

But Pierre St. Clair had me under lock and key. He followed me everywhere, even to the latrine, where he waited outside, tapping his foot.

I complained to my father, but my father, of course, took Pierre's side.

"You are the heir to this estate," my father said. "You must be groomed and educated."

"What if that is not my wish?" I shot back.

Father's eyebrows raised high. Other than that, his expression didn't change, which I knew meant he was angry, very angry indeed, and I'd best not anger him any further.

"I'll do as you say, Father," I said.

The truth was that I didn't want my father's life. He spent his days managing the estate and hosting other aristocrats at dull dinner parties. My mother wasn't about to take my side, either. She was always off at the royal court, rubbing elbows with the queen and attending fancy balls.

Our family was wealthy and wanted for nothing. And boring, so incredibly boring!

I was tired of trying to live up to my family's expectations. But what else was I to do? Without my father's money, I'd end up a beggar on the docks.

Unless I found a way to make my own fortune. Then I'd be free of this life. I'd answer to nobody. I could live life the way I wanted to.

But how could a young boy like me ever make his own fortune?

Voices drifted from the dining hall. I crouched on the stairwell, straining to listen.

My father was hosting another of his dinner parties.

And, as usual, I was not allowed to attend, instead having to eat with the servants in the back room. Despite saying he wanted to groom me, my father certainly didn't seem to want me around his friends.

Normally I didn't care to attend the dinner parties. But tonight was different. Tonight, we had a guest I desperately wanted to meet.

Earlier I had watched the guests arrive in their carriages. The last carriage arrived, and the man who stepped out looked nothing like the other guests. He was tall, bearded, and wore a long brown coat. As he turned toward the house, I caught a glimpse of his weathered, suntanned face. The face of a sailor.

Who could he be? I wondered. I'd never seen him on the docks, and he was too finely dressed to be an ordinary sailor.

My father stepped forward to greet him. "Jacques Cartier!" my father boomed. "A pleasure to meet you."

My heart sailed into my throat. Could it really be? The one and only Jacques Cartier, explorer of the New World across the ocean?

On the docks I'd heard stories of Cartier. Last year he had sailed across the Atlantic Ocean on King Francis's request, searching for a passage to Asia. He'd returned with two native princes and stories to tell.

He lived the life I wanted to lead. I longed to talk to him now that he was here in my own home as a dinner guest.

The only problem was I wasn't invited.

So instead, here I was, leaning over the railing, intent on every word from the dining room below.

Cartier was, of course, the guest of honor and the center of attention. *Maybe someday I, too, will have such stories to tell at the dinner table,* I thought.

"Tell us, sir, of your travels across the sea!" a woman's voice chimed.

Cartier's laugh boomed. "Most of my stories are not fit for a lady's ear," he said. "But I'll tell you that the journey was swift. The winds were favorable. But when we reached land, we found a very unfavorable place indeed. Barren and unlivable. And worse, cold winds batted against our ships without stopping. A passage to India seemed unlikely."

"So the voyage was a failure?" my father asked. He seemed a little too eager to believe the journey had failed.

I could hear the smile in Cartier's voice. "Not at all, sir. We turned south, and found paradise. A lusher land I've never seen. The natives were friendly and treated us as gods. And they told us …" Cartier paused for a long moment.

No one at the table made a single sound. I held my breath, waiting.

"They told us," Cartier continued, "of kingdoms of riches to the west!"

"And did you find these kingdoms?" my father asked. I could hear the frown in his voice.

"Not yet," Cartier said. "That is why I shall be returning soon. In two days' time, to be exact, if the winds are fair."

I realized I was still holding my breath, and I let it escape in a whoosh. Two days.

"My fleet of three ships lies in wait in the St. Malo harbor," Cartier finished.

The *Grande Hermine*, *Petite Hermine*, and the *Emerillon* — the three ships I'd seen and wondered at.

Fate was calling me. Fate had led me to the harbor that day, and fate had led Cartier to my home.

I knew what I had to do. I didn't even argue as my tutor St. Clair — not fate — tugged at my shoulders and led me away from the balcony.

For no one — not even my father — could tear me away from my destiny.

265
300
NW

Stowaway

The moon hung over the water, its light reflected into broken splinters. Waves crashed on the shore, roaring in my ears. I'd never realized the sea was so loud. Usually, the dock was filled with the hum and chatter of people, but tonight no one was here. Just me and the roaring sea.

Earlier, I'd slipped quietly from bed, careful not to wake Pierre St. Clair, who was asleep in the next room. I'd grabbed my clothes from under the bed where I'd stuffed them. Getting dressed was harder than I thought. I'd never dressed myself before. I'd always had servants to help me fasten buckles and knot strings. But somehow I managed, even though some of the buckles were askew.

Then I tiptoed down the stairs, unlatched the door, and stepped out into the night and my freedom. I had only the light of the moon to guide me to the harbor of St. Malo.

Now I stood staring at the silhouette of Cartier's fleet, anchored offshore. How could I sneak aboard? I couldn't swim. I had no raft.

The ships were tethered to the dock with long, thick ropes. I would have to climb along the ropes and pull myself to the deck.

Was I strong enough to do it? I had no choice. My fate was in my own hands, quite literally. I looked down at the soft skin of my palms, which had never held anything thicker than horses' reins. I flexed my fingers. I was ready. I had to be.

The *Petite Hermine*, the middle-sized ship, was the closest. Plus, Jacques Cartier would probably sail on the *Grande Hermine*. I didn't want him to discover me and realize I didn't belong. I had a better chance of avoiding discovery on the *Petite*.

The Petite *it is*, I thought, taking a deep breath.

I grasped the rope with both hands and lifted myself up, hooking my legs over the rope. So far, so good. Inch by inch, like a worm, I moved my body across the rope. *Don't look down,* I told myself. But I did anyway. Below me the water was thick and black. If I fell, I was doomed.

My arms shook. The skin of my palms felt like it was peeling off. But I had to keep going.

At last I neared the hull of the ship. Getting onto the ship would be the tricky part. I would have to drop my legs from the rope and swing over the railing of the ship, hoping my tired arms would be strong enough to hold my weight.

One. Two. Three. I loosened my legs and swung them back and forth to gain momentum. Then I let go.

I flailed wildly in midair for one long second. Then, *crash*! I fell onto the deck. The sound echoed like thunder.

Surely the entire crew had heard my ungraceful, noisy land. And surely I'd broken every bone in my body.

I lay on the deck, panic and excitement battling inside me. I thought I heard footsteps, but it was only my heart kicking my ribs. No one had heard me.

I was free. I was on board the *Petite Hermine*. And I was about to embark on the adventure of a lifetime.

But first, I had to hide. I lifted the latch that led below deck to the cargo hold. I dropped down into the blackness. I would stay hidden as long as it took, until we were so far from France and my father that there would be no turning back.

Somehow I fell asleep in the damp, dark hold, hiding behind a long crate. I woke to the ship swaying and my stomach lurching. We'd set sail!

I realized I hadn't taken a final look at St. Malo, my home. I might never see it again. I imagined how the city looked from the sea, its silhouette growing smaller and smaller while the sea got larger and larger. Until St. Malo disappeared forever.

I wiped my wet face. Surely I wasn't crying! No, it must be the dampness of the hold.

The ship reeled violently, and I knocked against the ship's side, stomach whirling. I wasn't seasick. No, it must be something I ate.

The thought of food made my stomach whirl again. I just needed sleep. I slid my body down the wall and closed my eyes. My head leaned against something soft. Mmm. A nice pillow.

Just as I was drifting to sleep, the pillow moved. I shot up straight. The pillow scurried away, its tail whapping me in the face. My warm, soft pillow was, in fact, a fat rat.

I wasn't scared of rats. No, not at all. I just didn't want to be sharing quarters with one. Or maybe two or three. I could hear nails skittering on wood. *When I find my fortune,* I thought, *I will rid the world of rats!*

285
300
NW
20
30
40
50

A Scoundrel, A Storm, and A Sailor's Life

"Get up, you scoundrel!" a voice bellowed.

I opened my eyes to find a man staring down at me. The candle he held illuminated his bulbous eyes and thick, reddish beard. His eyes narrowed. "Get up, you hear me?"

I scrambled to my feet, but the rocking ship threw me off balance, and I plunged against the sailor's shoulder. He shoved me backward and grabbed both my wrists with his meaty paw.

"We don't take kindly to stowaways," he growled, dragging me to the ladder. My rat friends scuttled away from our feet. The sailor pushed me up the ladder, and I had no choice but to climb.

I popped through the trapdoor into the bright sunshine. After countless hours in the dark hold, I couldn't adjust to the searing light. I was blind and staggering.

"What'd you find down there, Jean-Luc?" a voice hollered.

"Just some trash," my captor answered. He tossed his candle to the deck and grabbed my shoulders. "You know what we do with trash?" he hissed in my ear. "We toss it overboard!"

I felt the railing against my chest. I blinked. I could see again. And what I saw was the roiling sea below me, ready to swallow me up.

"Wait!" I cried. "Do you know who I am?"

"Don't care," muttered Jean-Luc.

"I am Samuel de la Loire, son of Royal Duke Michel de la Loire."

"By my knuckles you are," Jean-Luc said, shoving me against the railing again.

"My father will have you hanged if you throw me overboard," I said, in as confident a tone as I could muster.

Another sailor marched toward us. "Hold on, Jean-Luc," he said, eyeing me up and down. "He could be telling the truth. Look at his clothes! They aren't the clothes of a beggar."

Jean-Luc released his grip, giving me a small kick in the shin. His face was red as a grape. Anger steamed from his ears.

"Stay out of it, Henri," he barked.

"He's just a kid," Henri said. "And we could always use another pair of hands."

Jean-Luc kicked me again. "Aristocrat or not," he said, "you'll be getting no special treatment on this ship. Get to work!"

"Follow me," Henri said. As I followed him across the deck, I looked around. All ocean, as far as I could see. Adventure and fortune awaited me. I could taste it in the salty air.

I didn't imagine the seafaring life to be quite like this. I always thought a sailor's life was adventurous and thrilling — steering vessels through uncharted waters, bucking through the eye of a storm, watching sea creatures leap in the distance. But it was hard work. And a lot of it.

Henri showed me the ropes, so to speak. I was assigned about a hundred chores every day — scrub the deck, clean up after meals, oil the masts, man the winches. And I was at the beck and call of every sailor on board. I had to do whatever they told me.

And I was at the mercy of Jean-Luc Brouelle.

Jean-Luc took personal pleasure in ordering me about. "Aristocrat!" he barked one day. "Fetch the oil rags from the hold."

I dropped down into the hold. I searched and searched for the rags, but they were nowhere to be found.

When I returned to the deck, trembling in fear of a punishment, I found Jean-Luc laughing and tossing the missing oil rags into the air. "Couldn't find them, eh?" he chortled.

"Ease up," one of the other sailors called, but he was laughing too.

I looked over at the *Grande Hermine* as it bobbed in the waves, the smaller *Emerillon* behind it. If only I'd chosen one of those ships to sneak aboard, I wouldn't have to deal with Jean-Luc. I'd made the wrong decision.

It was the first of many.

The sea never rests, and neither did we. We slept only four hours at a time, and even then, my sleep was just a light doze on a hard mat. My body ached all over. After just a week at sea, my fine trousers were greased and stained, my nose sunburned, and my palms crisp with blisters.

I'll admit, I was miserable. I longed for my own bed, a cook to make my meals, and a hot, steamy bath. I even missed Pierre St. Clair's constant watching and worrying.

One night I was sleeping as peacefully as I could when the ship lurched forward, knocking me off my mat. All of a sudden, the crew was in a frenzy, leaping from their mats and shouting orders. I got to my feet. Hard, blustering wind and shards of rain battered my face. We were in a brutal storm.

I stood clinging to the railing, not knowing what to do, as the other sailors scurried around me. All I really wanted to do was drop down into the hold and huddle there until the storm was over. But I didn't want the crew to think I was scared.

"Lower the sails!" Henri cried.

He turned to see me standing helplessly, and he flung a rope in my direction. "Grab the end," he shouted. "And hold tight!"

I closed my hands around the end of slippery rope as Henri mounted the mast, the rope knotted around his waist.

The ship bucked under my feet. The soles of my boots were too smooth, meant for a gentleman, not a sailor. *Drat these boots!* I thought as I slid backward wildly, holding fast to the rope.

The rope snapped tight, and in the swirling rain I saw Henri look down at me, alarmed. The rope tugged him off balance, and he clung to the mast. "Let go!" he shouted.

But I couldn't let go. If I did, I'd be knocked over the side of the railing.

Should I save myself, or save Henri?

The ship pitched violently, and I slid along with it. I watched in horror as Henri tumbled from the mast to the deck below.

Too late, I let go of the rope.

And I tumbled end over end, over the railing and to my certain death.

The sky and sea closed around me, and the world turned black.

THE NEW WORLD AHEAD

Jean-Luc's face loomed over me like a demon. Yes, I was dead. And this was my punishment. I would spent eternity being tormented by Jean-Luc Brouelle.

He slapped my face with a wet palm. "Get up, Aristocrat!" he snarled.

I lifted my head and looked around. I was on the deck of the *Petite Hermine*. So I wasn't dead. But I was in big trouble.

"Henri?" I whispered. "Is he ... dead?"

"Takes more than a fall off a mast to kill me," Henri answered. His face appeared next to Jean-Luc's. "But *you'd* be dead if Jean-Luc hadn't fished you outta the water."

Jean-Luc snorted. "If I'd known it was you, I'd have let you go under. Where you belong."

I sat up and rubbed my eyes. Dawn was breaking over the water. The sea was calm, as if there'd never been a storm at all.

But something was missing. The sea around us was empty.

As if he'd read my mind, Henri said, "We lost sight of the other two ships. We're all alone out here now."

All alone.

The *Grande Hermine* could have capsized, taking Jacques Cartier and my dreams of fortune along with it.

"Will we turn back?" I asked.

Henri laughed. "You need to learn a thing or two about explorers. We never turn back. Not until we find what we are looking for."

Even though he'd saved me, Jean-Luc seemed to despise me even more now. He followed me around the ship, his heavy breath at my neck. "Aristocrat! Fetch me a drink."

"My name is Sam!" I muttered, but I did as I was told.

Worse, he often swiped food from my plate. "You owe me," he said.

So I went hungry most days.

Every night when I hunkered down on my mat to sleep, I stared up at the stars. Night after night, they didn't seem to change. *How long until we reach the New World?* I wondered. *If we ever do.*

One morning I was scrubbing the deck when I heard a shout. "Land ahead!" cried the lookout.

I rushed to the bow of the ship. Sure enough, up ahead a dark blob on the horizon grew larger as we sailed toward it.

At last, we'd reached the New World.

Cartier's ship, the *Grande Hermine*, bobbed in the distance, waiting for us.

265
300
10
20
30
40
50
60
NW

Royal Treatment

The land beneath my feet felt too solid. I was so used to the rocking of the ship that I couldn't keep my balance on the ground. I staggered, hearing Jean-Luc's snicker behind me. "Can't find your land legs, Aristocrat?" he said.

I ignored him. Instead, my eyes were pinned on Jacques Cartier, who was coming toward us. At his side were two young men, not much older than I. They wore the clothing of French sailors, but their skin was dark. *They must be the native chief's sons,* I thought.

Cartier greeted Mace Salobert, the captain of the *Petite Hermine*. Then his gaze settled on me. "Who's this boy?" he asked.

Jean-Luc spoke up. "Just a stowaway, Captain. I tried to throw him overboard—"

"My name is Samuel de la Loire," I interrupted, standing tall and straight. "I am the son of Royal Duke Michel de la Loire."

Cartier's eyes widened. He looked from me to Captain Salobert.

"Sam's been a good helper," Henri spoke up, coming toward us. I was glad he didn't mention that I'd almost killed him. "And he's courageous and passionate!"

Cartier sighed. "Does your father know where you are?" he asked.

"I'm sure he does now," I told him.

Cartier looked me straight in the eye. "One thing to understand, Sam," he said, "is that this isn't just a fun adventure. We are on a dangerous and important mission for the king."

"I understand, sir," I said.

"Very well, then," Cartier said. "From now on, you shall accompany me on the *Grande Hermine*. Then I can keep an eye on you. I wouldn't want anything to happen to the son of Royal Duke de la Loire."

"Yes, sir!" I replied, turning to follow him. I cast a grin into the scowling face of Jean-Luc Brouelle. "See, it pays to be an aristocrat!" I chuckled.

I felt his angry stare at my back as I boarded the *Grande Hermine*.

My grin stayed on my face as I stood at the ship's railing, looking west across the wide expanse of water and the smattering of islands. The sun, dipping into the horizon, shone bright as a gold coin against the water, like a fortune at the edge of the world.

Although I was now under Cartier's watch, I saw little of him. He spent his days bent over parchment paper, drawing maps of the islands we navigated around and sketching the marvelous birds and beasts we saw. Even the trees were different in the New World, larger and brighter in color.

Most of the other sailors on the *Grande* ignored me except to order me to fetch food or supplies for them. I didn't miss Jean-Luc pestering me, that's for sure, but I felt unnecessary and unwanted.

One day on deck I noticed the native chief's sons, Domagaya and Taignoagny, watching me. "You young boy!" Domagaya said in halting French.

I smiled at him. "I am an aristocrat. Like you. You are princes."

"Prince?" Taignoagny said slowly.

"It means your father is a leader," I said.

Domagaya nodded. "Our father is Donnacona, chief of Stadacona Iroquois."

"Iroquois?" I said, as slowly as Taignoagny had said "prince." The word felt awkward in my mouth. "That is your tribe?"

"We are home now," Domagaya said. He pointed west across the islands. "Can-a-da!"

"Cartier placed a symbol on the ground," Taignoagny said. He crossed his hands to make a *t* shape.

"A cross," I said.

"He said his god lives in the sky. And that Cartier is the leader on the land."

I nodded. "Yes! This land belongs to France now."

Taignoagny frowned. "No," he said. "Donnacona is the leader."

I didn't feel like arguing. I was more interested in fortune, not land. "Where is Saguenay?" I asked.

Domagaya grinned. "Saguenay! A great kingdom." He pointed to the ring I wore on my forefinger. "Much of this."

My heart quickened its beat. "Much silver? And gold?"

Domagaya nodded, still grinning.

"But where?" I asked. "Where is Saguenay?"

Taignoagny pointed toward the setting sun. "Far. You must travel far."

I will, I thought. *I will travel as long and as far as it takes to find my fortune.*

That night I lay awake thinking. My fortune was in reach. I imagined what I would do with my riches. I'd buy a grand house on the coast of France. My dinner parties wouldn't be boring like my father's. I wouldn't go to the king's court — I'd make the king come to me! I'd buy a fleet of ships and sail around the world, each trip a new adventure. My name would be on everyone's lips — Samuel de la Loire, the world's youngest explorer and the richest man in the world. *I have quite the life ahead of me,* I thought as I finally drifted to sleep.

285
300
NW
10
20
30
40
50
60

The Big Mistake

Something — or someone — was watching us. The hair on the back of my neck prickled. I scanned the trees that crept close to the shore. They were dark and silent.

We had dropped anchor alongside the Isle of Orleans, as Cartier had named it. Cartier had come ashore to explore. I was included in the expedition, of course, since Cartier kept me close by at all times.

I shook off the feeling and hurried to catch up with the others. Taignoagny and Domagaya were with us too. They kept looking around them, faces happy. I knew it was because they were home at last.

What would it feel like when I returned home? I wondered. *Would I be happy?* I wasn't sure. Everything here was so new and strange and exciting. *I won't go home until I have something to return with,* I told myself. *A treasure, a fortune. Gold and jewels from Saguenay.*

Behind me I heard branches snap. I whirled, hand on my sword, ready to draw.

A boy about my age stood in front of me. His eyes reflected the fear I felt as we stared at each other.

But other than that, we were nothing alike. His skin was deep bronze, and he was naked except for a breechcloth at his waist and a wooden spear in his hand. His hair dropped long down his back.

The boy's eyes flitted to my sword. I unleashed the sword and wagged it in the air.

Within a split second, the boy turned and sprinted down the shore, shouting in a language I couldn't understand. At his shout, a canoe rounded the bend. It was filled with five or six natives, all shouting.

I whacked the air with my sword.

The boy took another look back at my sword and leapt into the canoe. They rowed away furiously.

Domagaya ran past me, calling after them. When they heard their own language, they slowed their rowing.

Cartier grabbed my shoulder. "Do not draw your sword!" he said angrily. "We must maintain peace with the natives."

I dropped my sword into its sheath. "Sorry, sir," I mumbled. "I didn't mean to—"

"Enough!" Cartier said. He turned his attention to the group of natives, who had stepped ashore and were slowly approaching us.

Domagaya said something to the youngest of the group. The boy smiled widely. He pointed to Domagaya's jacket and laughed. Domagaya shrugged off the jacket and handed it to the boy, who held it up in wonder, still laughing.

"They didn't know us," Taignoagny told Cartier. "We are dressed like the French."

The group of natives followed us to our anchored ship, talking excitedly with Domagaya and Taignoagny. I wished I could understand their words and share their excitement. I realized then how lonely I felt, with no one my age to talk to and no friend in sight.

When we reached our ships, Cartier pulled me aside. His eyes still burned with anger. "Stay on the *Grande*," he said, "and don't come ashore unless I tell you to."

I knew I was being punished for brandishing my sword. Rage filled my chest. "My father—" I began.

"Your father is not here," Cartier interrupted. "Do as I say."

I turned and trudged to the *Grande*.

All afternoon I watched as canoe after canoe of natives came to our ships. Men, women, and children crowded the shore. Cartier handed out gifts — beads, combs, and small knives.

Even though I was upset at being stuck on the ship, I was entranced by the natives. Their language sounded like a song to my ears. They moved about so freely, not weighed down by heavy clothing. I'd never seen so much skin before, and I felt embarrassed in my long jacket and trousers.

The next day Chief Donnacona came to visit. He stood regally among his people, wearing a long robe around his shoulders. Feathers poked from his hair. He looked like a king.

Domagaya and Taignoagny rushed to their father, and he caught them up in a hug. As I watched them embrace, I wondered if I would ever see my father again. What would our reunion be like? Would he hug me? Or scold me? I missed him. I missed home.

Unable to watch anymore, I went below deck and huddled against a barrel, out of sight. I stayed there until the tears stopped dribbling down my cheeks.

265
NW

THE GIFT

Our three ships sailed up the St. Lawrence River to another river, the St. Charles, where we dropped anchor across from the great Iroquois village of Stadacona. Here we would spend the winter.

But first, Cartier wanted to explore upriver to another great village, Hochelaga, in the hopes of finding the way to Saguenay. He would take 50 men with him.

"Please, sir, will you take me with you?" I asked, feeling like a child begging for sweets.

Cartier gave a quick shake of his head. "No, Sam. You must stay here."

I turned away, but not before he saw my crestfallen face. "Your mission here is just as important," he told me. "Stay here, and help build our winter fort, Fort Holy Cross."

But to me, nothing was as important as finding Saguenay, the kingdom of gold.

I vowed I would find it, with or without Cartier.

The Iroquois did not want Cartier to go to Hochelaga, either. Hundreds of natives came to the riverbank to see us, but Chief Donnacona, Taignoagny, and Domagaya stood apart, watching us solemnly.

The next day the natives gathered on the riverbank again, but this time they danced and sang in celebration. "I will go to greet them," Cartier said, stepping into a canoe. I hopped in after him, thinking he would tell me to stay on our side of the river. But he paid me no attention, and we rowed across the river to the natives.

Donnacona greeted us. Then he turned to his people gathered behind him and drew one little girl, about ten years old, and two younger boys forward.

"These children are a gift to you," Taignoagny explained. "If you promise to travel no farther."

Cartier shook his head. "My king commanded me to travel as far as possible. I will go to Hochelaga."

Taignoagny and Donnacona spoke at length, and then Taignoagny turned back to Cartier. "You must accept these children as gifts."

I motioned for the children to get into the canoes. The two boys leaped in eagerly, but the little girl trembled with fear.

"We are nice people," I told her. I knew she couldn't understand my words, but I hoped she understood my meaning. "We won't harm you. You will live with us now."

I helped her into the canoe, and she huddled against me as we rowed back to our ships. The two boys fell silent too, watching their home disappear behind us. Even when we had boarded the *Grande* and given them food and a place to sleep, the children still huddled together, scared.

I found Cartier in his quarters belowdecks. "We should give the children back," I told him.

Cartier shook his head. "The children are gifts," he said, "and we cannot return them. It would anger the entire village." He paused and then added, "You have a lot to learn, Sam. You're just a child yourself."

I strode out of his room. I was tired of being told I had a lot to learn. I was tired of being treated like a child. I would take matters into my own hands.

That night I gathered as many items as I could find — a fallen leaf, a walnut, a handful of dirt, a candle, and a knife — and sat next to the little girl. She looked up at me, her eyes watery. "Sam," I said, pointing to my chest.

"Sam," she repeated slowly.

I pointed to her. "What is your name?"

"Asfomahagny."

She giggled when I tried to pronounce it. She pointed to the moon above us. *"Assomaha,"* she said.

"Moon," I said, pointing to the moon and then to her. When she nodded, I said, "I will call you Moon."

Then I spread the items one by one on the deck. I asked her the name of the leaf. *"Hoga,"* she said. The walnut was *quahoya*, the knife *agoheda*. When we ran out of items, I pointed to the sky, where the stars spread above us. "Stars," I said.

"Stgnehoha," she answered.

As we spoke, I thought of the New World, and how different it was from my own. Then I shook my head. *No*, I thought. *We are all of the same world. We just have different words.*

Cartier's Quest

Jean-Luc Brouelles swung his knapsack as he shouldered past me. He flashed me a toothy grin. "See you later, Aristocrat," he said.

"Where are you going?" I asked, although I was certain I already knew. He had been asked to join Cartier's expedition to Hochelaga.

Jean-Luc's grin grew wider. "I guess all your explorer dreams are squashed now," he said. "Have fun holding down the fort while I go off to find your treasure!"

He strode toward the *Emerillon*, still laughing, while I stared after him.

All day we'd been preparing the *Emerillon* for Cartier's departure. The *Emerillon* was smaller than the other two ships and could navigate shallow rivers more easily. Cartier's group would be gone at least a month, so we loaded the hold with food, supplies, and, of course, gifts for the natives.

I considered sneaking aboard the *Emerillon* like I'd done in St. Malo. But I knew Cartier would send me back. And when I saw Moon standing silently, watching me carry supplies to the ship, her eyes wide, I knew I was needed here. Moon needed me.

"I don't know why Jean-Luc hates me so much," I grumbled to Henri. "What did I ever do to him?"

Henri shrugged. "He had a hard life as a kid. He grew up an orphan on the streets of St. Malo. He probably envies your upbringing in a wealthy home."

"At least he was free to do what he wanted with his life," I said. "I had to run away from home to find my freedom."

Henri nodded. "Maybe you and Jean-Luc are more alike than you think."

I shuddered. "No way."

As the *Emerillon* sailed out of sight, I vowed not to think about Jean-Luc. Or Cartier. Or the treasures they might find.

Instead, I focused on helping set up Fort Holy Cross — putting up walls, hunting game, gathering berries, building cooking fires, and taking my turn at making meals for the crew. Whenever I could, I played with the two little native boys. And I helped Moon learn my language so I could learn hers.

With her help, maybe someday I'd find the riches I was looking for. *Henyosco.* Gold.

My days were so busy that I didn't realize how fast time slipped by. After we'd built the walls of the fort, we dug a deep moat around it. Then we placed cannons on each wall.

I couldn't understand why we'd put up cannons. Who was our enemy?

When I asked Henri, he answered with a shrug. "We are in wild lands, among wild people. We never know when we might be attacked."

I thought of the Iroquois I knew — Domagaya, Taignoagny, Moon, and Donnacona. They'd always been friendly to us. They didn't seem like wild people. They'd done nothing but help us.

Cartier's expedition returned in the middle of October, amidst freezing drizzle and winds. I was somewhat relieved to see they bore no treasures. They hadn't found Saguenay.

I grinned at Jean-Luc as he disembarked from the *Emerillon*. He was wearing his usual scowl.

"Empty hands, Jean-Luc?" I said. "No treasure?"

"Not yet," he answered as he passed me. Then he turned and leaned into my ear. "But I know the way."

I didn't believe him, not then. But soon I would stumble upon the truth.

Cartier didn't seem pleased with the cannons, either, but he didn't protest. "I am no longer sure of our friendship with the Stadacona Iroquois," I overheard him telling Henri. "And I have heard of other tribes who are even more warlike."

I couldn't help but feel resentment. He hadn't taken me with him to Hochelaga because I had drawn weapons against the natives. But now he seemed fine with pointing our cannons in their direction.

That night I found Cartier in his quarters alone, bent over his desk, writing. "Monsieur Cartier," I began.

He looked up at me, his face bright in the candlelight. "Yes, Sam?"

I cleared my throat and began. "One day, I would like to be an explorer as great as you," I said. "I want to learn from you. Will you tell me everything you saw?"

Cartier smiled and motioned for me to sit. Then he told me all he had seen. "The land is fair and a good place for a French settlement. The village of Hochelaga is larger than Stadacona, and the natives are friendly. We have made a fine claim for France."

I leaned forward. "And what of Saguenay, the kingdom of riches? Did you find it?"

Cartier shook his head. "No. But just before Hochelaga, there is a river. The chief of Hochelaga told me it leads to Saguenay."

I peered at the maps Cartier had been drawing. He saw my gaze and flipped the pages over. "We won't search for Saguenay on this journey, Sam. Winter is coming. And in the spring, we will sail back to France."

"But … how can you return without gold?" I asked. "Won't King Francis be angry?"

"No. My mission was to find a Northwest Passage to Asia. And the St. Lawrence River may lead to the passage. As for the gold …" he paused. "I have proof, which I will take back to the king."

Proof? I glanced quickly around Cartier's quarters. I saw no gold.

"Finding Saguenay is *my* mission, not yours, Sam." Cartier stood, his voice stern. "Now leave me."

I left without another word.

Escape Plan

The stars glittered like jewels in the sky. One star seared across the sky. A shooting star. A jewel, ready to fall into my palm.

"Sam?" Moon's small voice startled me. I turned to see tears glazing her cheeks.

"What's the matter, Moon?"

She pointed across the river. "Home. You take me?"

The meaning of her words sank in. She wanted me to help her escape. Could I? Could I betray Cartier?

I glanced at the cannons. By helping Moon, I'd not only betray Cartier. I'd be risking my life.

I looked down at her sniffling face. She longed to return home, just as I, months ago, had longed to leave home. I knew how it felt to have such longing.

"Yes, Moon," I told her. "I will help you."

I had a plan. It wasn't a good plan, but it was better than nothing. I decided it would be easier to get caught at night, when guards were on the lookout and Fort Holy Cross was silent. But during the day, the camp bustled with noise. Each man was intent on his duties. No one would notice if Moon quietly slipped away.

Once anyone noticed she was gone, she'd be safely in Stadacona.

But first I had to distract them, even at the risk of my own life.

A few days later, I saw my chance. Much of the crew was out hunting, and the rest of us were busy with daily duties.

I told Moon the plan. We went over it until I was sure she understood. "Wait until you hear shouting," I told her.

Then I rejoined Henri to help skin a deer. As we were working, I suddenly stopped and tilted my head. "Did you hear that?" I said. "Sounds like a war whoop."

Before Henri had a chance to respond, I scurried to the lookout and climbed to the top. "Over there!" I cried.

A few crew members rushed toward me.

"Whoa," I said. I pretended to lose my balance, and then I toppled over the lookout. I hit the ground at a roll.

I didn't stop rolling until I hit the moat. "Help!" I cried, as the water seized me. "I can't swim!"

Between my gasps for air, I heard the sound of the gate opening and footsteps rushing toward me.

Strong arms pulled me from the water. Henri. I knew he'd come to my aid.

I wiped moat water from my face and looked up at the other crew members.

"What did you hear?" one asked, jerking me to my feet.

"Over there," I answered weakly, pointing to the trees. "I thought I heard yelling. And then something crashing …"

Just then, like a miracle, two deer emerged from the woods to stare at us before bounding away, twigs breaking under their hooves.

Henri sighed. "Just deer," he said. "When will you stop almost drowning?"

"Guess I better learn to swim," I said lightly as we trudged back into the fort.

By now Moon had slipped out of the open gate in the midst of the chaos, swum across the moat, and escaped to her home.

As we closed the gate behind us, I saw Jean-Luc watching me, as though he knew.

Moon's disappearance went unnoticed for one whole day. That entire day, I felt wracked with both worry and relief. "She's just a child," I told myself whenever worry rose in me. "She's of no value to Cartier."

Cartier questioned me about her disappearance. "You were close to the child," he said. "Did you plan her escape?"

I shook my head emphatically. "No, sir," I said, trying to sound as convincing as possible. "Why would I want to lose my friend? She must have slipped away unnoticed when the gate opened."

He sighed. "I know what I need to do. I need to visit Stadacona and retrieve her."

"But, sir," I stuttered, "she doesn't want to be here!"

"She was a gift to us," Cartier said firmly. "We

will present her to King Francis as a symbol of our friendship with the Iroquois."

I couldn't argue. I could only hope.

My heart plummeted to my feet when Cartier sailed into Fort Holy Cross with Moon at his side. I couldn't meet her eyes. Instead, I turned away as she ran toward the two other "gifts" — the small Iroquois boys.

Later that night Moon crept to my cot, where I lay awake. She whispered a string of Iroquois words and patted my shoulder. I didn't understand everything she said, but I knew she was saying thank you for helping her go back to Stadacona to say goodbye. "France," she added, her toothy grin catching the moonlight. "Big adventure!"

Even though she seemed happy, I still felt terrible for the failed escape.

I didn't know then that by trying to save her, I saved myself.

285
300
NW
10
20
30
40
50
60

X Marks the Spot

Winter crashed down on us. The wind never stopped blowing. Snow fell around us into great white mounds. Winter in France had never been so cold. I found myself longing for my bedroom, with its fireplace and the hot baths the servants always drew for me. I closed my eyes and imagined myself sinking into steaming water until I could feel the heat on my skin. That helped a bit.

Jean-Luc had a newfound pleasure of clumping snow into balls and throwing them, mostly at me. He laughed uproariously as I brushed the snow off my head and chest.

I tried throwing snowballs back at him, but I always missed.

My head hurt. My teeth felt like they were about to fall out. In fact, one did.

Worse, my legs and arms turned purple and black. And I ached like the whole world was pressing down on me.

I was sick. Most of us were. We had the pestilence, as Cartier called it. Most likely it was scurvy, a sailor's disease.

Moans rose from Holy Cross as we all huddled in our crude shelters under blankets. One sailor died, then another and another. We buried the bodies under the snow because the ground was too frozen to dig graves.

I hoped I wouldn't be next.

Cartier did what he could. But there wasn't much he could do. We were in a strange land, with little food and no medicine. I often saw him staring up at the sky, as if imploring God to save us.

I wasn't quite as ill as the others. I was young, so I had more strength. But still I ached. And my moans often joined those of the others.

One night, I couldn't sleep. Sometimes walking helped the aches, so I wrapped a fur blanket around me and stepped from the shelter.

The night was clear and cold, and a ghostly moon threw light from the sky.

I nearly stumbled over a bundle lying in the snow. The bundle turned over, and a face looked up at me.

"Jean-Luc! What are you doing out here?" I gasped.

He stared as though trying to figure out who I was. Then he grinned, his usual wicked grin minus a few teeth. "You!" he hissed. "Aristocrat! I saw you. I know what you did."

I knelt down and tugged at his shoulder. "You are sick," I said. "Come back to the shelter, out of the cold."

He shook his head as he sat up. Flakes of snow flew from his beard. "I have to tell," he whispered.

My heart froze. I remembered Jean-Luc lurking and watching me after Moon escaped. Did he know?

"Tell what, Jean-Luc?"

"I have a secret," he said. "I have to tell you. Even though I never liked you much, we are connected. I saved you from death." He paused, chest heaving. "And now I am dying."

"You aren't dying," I said. "Come back to shelter."

"I don't want my secret to die with me." He spread his arms in front of him.

Then I saw, lighted by the moon, what lay in front of Jean-Luc. A map. Drawn into the snow.

"Hochelaga," whispered Jean-Luc. "The natives at Hochelaga told me the way. The way to Saguenay."

I stared at the map as Jean-Luc traced it with a blue finger. "I was always jealous of you. You had everything I wanted — a home, a family. But you left it all." He gave a hoarse laugh. "Still, I see your desire. You want to explore. You want your own wealth. And to find fame."

I looked from the map to Jean-Luc. Despite the cold, sweat peppered his forehead.

"You are the only one," he said. "I feel your desire. You will find it. If I live, you will share it with me."

He turned to me and gripped my arm. "You promise?"

I nodded, and his grip grew tighter. "Yes, I promise," I told him.

He swiveled and leaned over the map. "Follow the St. Lawrence." He pointed to a curved line etched deep into the snow. His finger moved to a shape of a hill, with rocks like a crown atop it. "This is King's Mound. After King's Mound, you will see a small river. And then there! X marks the spot."

With that, he slumped to the ground.

I stared at the map so hard that when I blinked, I could still see it in my eyelids.

I rolled Jean-Luc over, careful not to smudge the map. He was still breathing. I slapped his cheek, and he opened his eyes. With all my strength, I propped him into a sitting position. "Help!" I called.

At the sound of running footsteps, I shouted again and waved. Two sailors who hadn't fallen sick rushed to us and pulled Jean-Luc to his feet. They staggered with him to the shelters.

I followed, but not until I took one last look at the map and then stomped it out until it disappeared. No one would ever know.

285
300
NW

The Way to Saguenay

Every night I dreamed of the map. Even during the day, I dreamed of it. The map that would seal my fortune.

As I recovered, Jean-Luc got sicker and sicker. I helped Cartier tend to the ill, and whenever I knelt next to Jean-Luc, he grabbed my wrist and pulled me close to his face. "Find it," he said.

"I will," I promised. "Believe me, I will."

I thought Jean-Luc would certainly die. But help came just in time, in the shape of Domagaya.

Domagaya marched into Fort Holy Cross one day in late December. He'd been ill with pestilence, he explained. He asked if any of us were ill.

"Just one," Cartier lied. I knew he didn't want Domagaya to know so many of us were ill, and that 25 were already dead. He was afraid the natives would attack us.

"I know a cure," Domagaya said. "I will bring to you!"

Later, Domagaya returned with strips of tree bark. "Boil these," he said. "And drink. Women from Stadacona will gather more for you."

The cure worked. Everyone recovered. The Stadacona Iroquois had saved us.

Winter wore on. I studied the map in my mind. The way to Saguenay was long, and I knew I wouldn't survive the journey in this harsh winter. I would have to wait until spring.

I saw Jean-Luc watching me. Coming so near to death seemed to have changed him. He no longer hurled snowballs or insults at me. He rarely spoke and always did as he was told.

But I wasn't sure I could trust him. I knew he was just waiting for his chance to slip out of camp and find

Saguenay for himself.

I just had to beat him to it.

"Jean-Luc is gone," Henri told me one day in late April. The air had warmed suddenly, and the snow was melting into muddy puddles at our feet.

But at Henri's words, I felt frozen. "Gone? Where?"

Henri shrugged. "Disappeared. He took off in the middle of the night. No one knows where he went."

But I knew. He was on his way to Saguenay.

I had to follow him. I had to reach Saguenay first. If I found it — *when* I found it — my name would go down in history. And I'd be rich.

But if Jean-Luc found Saguenay first, it would be his name on everyone's lips.

I couldn't bear it.

I had little time to prepare. I thought about everything I would need. Food, as much as I could carry. A knife. A blanket, for the nights were still cold. And what I needed most was a shortcut. If I found a shortcut, I could overtake Jean-Luc.

I crept to Cartier's quarters and stole a piece of parchment from his desk. Using his inkwell and pen, I drew the map. I studied it long and hard, looking for a shortcut.

Then it dawned on me. I didn't need a shortcut. I needed a canoe.

The easiest option would be to steal one of our canoes. Well, not steal, but borrow. Because I'd return to Holy Cross with much more than a canoe.

But I knew that if a canoe was missing, the crew would know where I was headed, and they'd follow me.

It was much safer to leave camp, go as far as my legs would carry me, and then build my own canoe. No one would try to find me. No one had tried to find Jean-Luc, after all.

Except that Jean-Luc was an orphan with no family. And I was the son of an aristocrat, with a powerful father who would skin Cartier's hide if anything happened to me. For that reason, Cartier might send the crew to search for me.

I had to take my chances.

I couldn't let Jean-Luc get any farther ahead than he already was. I had to leave as soon as night fell.

Quickly, I turned my map over and sketched a canoe. I knew I could build it. I'd watched shipbuilders in St. Malo building much larger boats. I'd learned their techniques just by watching them.

That night, when Holy Cross was silent, I crept out of camp, armed with a hatchet, a knife, a pail, and food. And courage. I needed a lot of that.

And then I ran.

265
300
NW
10
20
30
40
50
60

The Lone Journey

I don't know how far I ran. All I know is I didn't stop for hours. I focused on the beating of my feet against the banks of the river to drown out any spooky sounds coming from the trees. Whenever I imagined a bear attacking me, I replaced the image with a chest of gold. And I kept plunging forward.

At dawn I stopped running. My eyes scanned the banks for fallen trees. At last I found what I was looking for. Almost like a miracle, a tree larger than any I'd ever seen had fallen right in my path.

With my hatchet, I chopped the tree into a log about seven feet long. Then I hollowed out the inside. With my knife, I whittled both ends to come to a point. I used the rest of the tree to carve out two long oars.

It sounds easy, but believe me, it wasn't. It took me until the next morning to finish. I barely stopped to eat, and I only slept when the moon slipped beneath the clouds and it was too dark to see.

As the morning sun spread out behind me, I stepped into the canoe and pushed away from shore.

The current pushed me back several feet. I'd forgotten about the current. I'd have to row against it the whole way.

More determined than ever, I slapped my oars into the water and began my journey.

I tried not to think about how alone I was. But out here, under a sweeping sky, with no sounds other than the squawk of birds and the rushing of water, it was hard to forget. I felt like the only person in the entire world.

After a full day of rowing, I would pull the canoe onto the shore and hunker down in it for the night, covered with a blanket. My stomach was raw with hunger. I rationed my food supply. I gnawed on the salted meat in my pack and a few berries I gathered, but it was never enough. I tried to catch fish, but they were sparse and hard to catch in the deep waters of the St. Lawrence River.

Had I made a mistake trying to find Saguenay on my own? Had my greediness led me out here, on a path to my death?

No, I told myself. *It's only the hunger talking. Keep pressing on.*

So I did. And at last, I saw a hill rising in the distance, topped with a crown of boulders. King's Mound. My heart tumbled with excitement. I was close now.

The river to Saguenay lay just past King's Mound, according to Jean-Luc's map. But as I rowed past the mound, I saw nothing. Nothing but more trees.

I unfolded the map from my pocket. *After King's Mound, turn south on the river,* Jean-Luc had said.

But there was no river.

I told myself to keep going. But after another full day of rowing, I found nothing.

Jean-Luc had been lying.

The truth hit me like a mad wind. How could I have believed him? I'd thought he was telling me his dying secret. But instead, it was a trick.

He was probably sitting on a golden throne in Saguenay this very minute, laughing at his cruel joke.

I slapped the oars against the water. Tears streamed down my face. I was angry at myself. And at Jean-Luc. And Cartier. And my father. And everyone in the world.

I lifted the oars over my head and slammed them into the water. The canoe spun with the force of my movement. I flew backward against the end of the boat and fell into the water.

I was doomed. I didn't know how to swim. *I'll die out here,* I thought as I waved my arms, kicking against the current. *And no one will remember my name. Even my father will forget me someday.*

As I coughed up a mouthful of water, I envisioned Jean-Luc standing on the shore, laughing. *I'll show him,* I thought. *I will survive.*

The canoe barreled toward my splashing, gasping body. I grabbed it and held tight, then kicked for the shore.

My feet touched the ground. I'd made it.

I heaved my body toward the shore, shivering and wheezing.

Then a terrible thing happened. The canoe slipped out of my wet, frozen hands. The current caught it and spun it downriver. Within seconds it was out of sight.

Along with my knife, my hatchet, and my pack of food.

Now I was really doomed.

265
300
NW

Guiding Star

I straggled along the shore, trying to calculate how long it would take to walk back to Holy Cross. Maybe, just maybe, I could find a fallen log to use as a raft.

I trudged into the woods, scanning the trees.

Then my stomach dropped to my toes. I hadn't found a fallen tree. Instead I'd found a pair of eyes, watching me.

Our eyes met for a brief second. Then the girl turned and ran, crashing through branches.

"Wait!" I called. "Please, help me!"

I searched my mind for the words Moon had taught me. Nothing was useful, but I gave it a try anyway. "Ship! Deer! River!" I yelled in Iroquois.

The girl stopped. Slowly she turned around, still eyeing me warily. She said something I couldn't understand.

"Boat," I said. "River." I tucked my arms around myself and shivered. Then I rubbed my belly. "Food," I said. I pointed to my chest. "Sam."

Her eyes widened. She approached me, her footsteps slow and silent. "Sam?" she said. "You help Moon?"

I bobbed my head up and down. "Yes! Moon is my friend."

She grinned. "Thank you," she said. "Moon is my—" she finished with a word I didn't know. At my puzzled look, she said, "Sister-sister."

"Moon is your sister?"

She shook her head. "Sister-sister."

"Cousin?" I said in French.

The girl shrugged too. She pointed at her chest. "I am Lrigsnotsagaya."

"Lrig ... what?"

She giggled. "Call me Star. Like moon. But not quite moon."

Star led me along the river, talking the whole time. I only understood bits and pieces. She said her family was happy I tried to help Moon. And now she would help me. She told me that she was with a hunting party, and that they had canoes and would take me back to Fort Holy Cross.

I couldn't believe my luck.

Fort Holy Cross was empty. Everyone was gone. Absolutely everyone.

Cartier had sailed back to France. Without me.

Star tried to comfort me as I doubled over, trying not to cry.

"You live with us now," she said. "Until your people return."

Later I learned that Cartier and the crew had sailed for France suddenly. He'd taken Chief Donnacona, Domagaya, Taignoagny, and a dozen other Iroquois with him. Moon was gone too. Cartier had promised to return next spring.

I wondered if Jean-Luc was still out there somewhere, searching for Saguenay.

I took my first step into the village of Stadacona, my new home. The village was surrounded by a log wall, not much different than Fort Holy Cross.

But the rest was quite different. The Iroquois lived in long, wooden houses with arched roofs. Several families shared one home.

Star led me into the longhouse she shared with her family. The smoke from the hearths inside the longhouse burned my eyes. I followed her down a long central hallway, dodging running children and women frying fish over the hearth. Then Star pointed to a mat on one side of the hallway. There I would sleep next to her two brothers.

At first the longhouse seemed cramped. But I got used to having so many people — nearly one hundred — under one roof. I even learned all their names. And I learned the truth about Saguenay.

Saguenay didn't exist.

I thought I'd be shocked, but I wasn't. Deep in my heart, I think I'd known all along.

Star explained that Saguenay was a legend, a made-up story the Iroquois told to entertain one another. Domagaya and Taignoagny had probably told the story to Cartier to make sure he'd bring them home.

"Maybe Saguenay is somewhere," Star shrugged. "But no one knows where."

My People

All that summer I earned my keep. I fished with other Iroquois men. I went on hunting parties where I speared my first deer. I'd never tasted meat so good.

I shed my French clothing and wore only a buckskin breechcloth at my waist and moccasins on my feet. I grew my hair into a long tail down my back. My skin browned from the sun. I'd never felt so free, so alive. I was Iroquois.

But still, as winter melted into spring, I stood at the edge of the St. Lawrence River, eyes turned east, waiting to see Cartier's ships on the horizon, coming to bring me home.

But Cartier never came.

I no longer thought about gold and riches. Gold didn't matter in Stadacona. Here we shared everything. Food, furs, fires, and songs. Here we were all rich.

Star married a young man from the village, and at the wedding we feasted, danced, and sang to the heavens. She had a baby, a boy she named Sam. As he grew, Sam chased after me, delighting in calling me Sam. "Sam!" he'd shout.

"Sam!" I'd shout back, and he'd giggle.

"You should marry too," Star told me. But I shook my head. "Why not?" she asked.

"Someday," I told her, tears catching in my throat, "someday I want to go home."

I thought she'd argue that Stadacona was my home, but she didn't. She seemed to understand.

One spring day, five years later, I was fishing in the river with my Iroquois brothers when one of them gave a shout. "Look!" he cried. He pointed down the river.

I saw a tall ship's mast silhouetted against the sky.

"Your people!" my brother said.

"My people," I said, my words catching in my throat.

Cartier didn't recognize me. I, along with my brothers and others from Stadacona, had rowed to the *Grande Hermine* where it lay in anchor. We wanted to greet Cartier and welcome Chief Donnacona home.

Cartier invited us onto the ship, and I stood next to my brothers to greet him.

Cartier's eyes passed over me without a second glance. "Donnacona is dead," he said in halting Iroquois.

My brothers fell to the ground in grief, wailing. I glanced around the ship, hoping to see Domagaya, Taignoagny, and Moon. But they were nowhere to be seen.

Cartier explained that his journey had been delayed five years due to a war with Spain. In the meantime, the other Iroquois had decided to stay in France. "They are now wealthy lords and ladies!" he said. But his smile was false. I knew he was lying. They were dead.

And Moon, my little friend, was dead too.

I swallowed back my sorrow and stepped forward. "Jacques Cartier," I said. I searched my mind for French words. I'd been speaking Iroquois so long that French felt strange in my mouth. "I would like you to take me home. To St. Malo."

Cartier frowned at me.

"I am Samuel de la Loire," I went on. "Son of Royal Duke Michel de la Loire."

He stared at me, stunned. "Sam? We thought you were dead! Your father is heartbroken."

"That is why I must return," I said. "I want to see my father. I want to go home."

FORTUNE

Jacques Cartier's mission was still to find gold and riches for the king. But he had another mission too. This time he'd brought men to settle the area. For good.

King Francis had released hundreds from prison to build a French settlement on the St. Lawrence River. Prisoners would make good settlers, the king thought. They could prepare the land for other French to follow. And if they died, no one would miss them.

As the prisoners filed off the ships and onto the site of their new settlement, Charlesbourg-Royal, I was filled with dread. What would happen to the Iroquois if the French took over the land? Would they be able to live peacefully side-by-side?

Then I saw a sight that stopped my breath.

Jean-Luc Brouelle was one of the prisoners.

I visited Charlesbourg-Royal nearly every day. I didn't want to help them settle the land, but I wanted to help maintain peace between the French and Iroquois.

Finally, I got my chance to confront Jean-Luc.

I stepped in front of him as he was hauling a crate from the ship. "Jean-Luc Brouelle," I said.

He looked me up and down.

"Samuel de la Loire," I told him. "Aristocrat."

His eyes bored into mine, as if trying to see if I was telling the truth. Then his face slumped. He tried to edge around me, but I blocked his way.

"You tricked me," I said. "I thought you were a dying man telling me a secret. But you were just a liar."

"I paid my price," Jean-Luc said, his eyes lowered. "When I returned to St. Malo, I had nothing. So I stole. And then got thrown into prison."

"And did you ever tell Cartier of your trickery?" I asked.

Jean-Luc shook his head. "I didn't really have a map, but I didn't mean to trick you," he said. "I waited in the woods for you to follow. I thought we could find Saguenay together. But you never came. So I went back to Holy Cross, but you weren't there." He chewed his lip, glancing around without meeting my eyes. "I thought you were dead. I didn't want you to die. I've been sick with guilt ever since."

"Why did you trick me, Jean-Luc? Instead of just telling me the truth?" I had to know. I had to hear his reason, although I knew it already.

"I wanted to teach you a lesson. You thought you could come here to the New World and make a fortune. Bigger than the fortune you've already got. It just didn't seem fair to me. Some of us have nothing, not a single penny."

"I did find a fortune," I told him. As his eyebrows raised, I went on. "But it's the kind you can't see."

His eyes finally met mine. He nodded in understanding.

"Thank you, Jean-Luc," I told him and turned to walk away.

"Wait!" he said. He lowered his voice. "The natives we brought back to France — Domagaya, Taignoagny, and the others. They aren't lords and ladies. They all died."

I nodded. I'd already suspected as much.

"Except one," Jean-Luc went on. "The little girl you called Moon."

"Moon is alive?" I said.

He nodded. "She's in St. Malo." With that, he turned and shuffled away.

Cartier didn't believe me when I told him Saguenay didn't exist. He continued to search for the kingdom. His crew found gold and diamonds along the shores of the St. Lawrence River. They gathered as much as they could and loaded the ships with their jewels to send back to France.

I knew the jewels weren't real. The gold was just a shimmering rock called iron pyrite, and the diamonds were quartz. And I was right. The following year, Cartier would present the jewels to King Francis only to be disappointed and shamed. He'd found only fool's gold.

Meanwhile my adopted Iroquois tribe was unhappy about the settlement. Our new chief called for attacks on the French to drive them away.

I knew it was time to say goodbye. I prepared to set out for Charlesbourg-Royal and board the *Saint-Georges* bound for France.

Star didn't cry as we embraced a final time. She only whispered, "Find Moon."

"I will," I promised.

As the *Saint-Georges* sailed down the river, I took one look back at Stadacona and the New World, the wild land that had been my home for so long. Then I turned my face to the east. To France. I was finally going home.

My pockets were empty, but my heart was filled with riches no one could ever take from me.

And that is how I became the world's youngest explorer. And the richest man in the world.

About the Author

Jessica Gunderson grew up in the small town of Washburn, North Dakota. She has a bachelor's degree from the University of North Dakota and an MFA in Creative Writing from Minnesota State University, Mankato. She has written more than 50 books for young readers. Her book *Ropes of Revolution* won the 2008 Moonbeam Award for best graphic novel. She currently lives in Madison, Wisconsin, with her husband and cat.

Making Connections

1. Even though Sam doesn't find gold and jewels, he calls himself the richest man in the world. What does he mean?

2. Why does Jean-Luc bully Sam? Do you think Sam forgives him?

3. How does Sam's character change throughout the book?

4. Why do you think Sam returns to France at the end? What are his reasons?

5. What do you think happens to Sam after he returns to France? Write an epilogue describing his life after he returns.

6. In your own words, describe the reasons King Francis sent Jacques Cartier to explore the New World. Do these reasons change when Cartier returns near the end of the book?

Glossary

aristocrat (uh-RIS-tuh-krat)—someone who is born into royalty and is usually wealthy and powerful

askew (uh-SKYOO)—crooked or off-center

breechcloth (BREECH-clawth)—a cloth worn around the waist

bulbous (BUHL-buhs)—resembling a bulb in being rounded or swollen

current (KUHR-uhnt)—the part of a body of water moving in a certain direction

estate (e-STAYT)—a large country house on a large piece of land

hold (HOHLD)—the interior of a ship belowdecks in which cargo is often stored

hull (HUHL)—the frame or body of a ship

mast (MAST)—a long pole that rises from the bottom of a ship or boat and supports the sails and rigging

moat (MOHT)—a deep, wide trench around a fort or castle that is usually filled with water

monsieur (muh-SOO-ur)—used as a title equal to "Mister" for a Frenchman

pestilence (PEH-stuh-lenss)—a contagious or infectious disease that spreads quickly and is often fatal

royal court (ROY-uhl KORT)—the residence of a king or queen

stowaway (STOH-uh-way)—an unregistered passenger; one who sneaks aboard a ship

tutor (TOO-tur)—a teacher or instructor

winch (WINCH)—a machine that has a roller on which a cable, chain, or rope is wound for pulling or lifting; winches are used to raise and lower sails and anchors

Read more about the people involved in the exploration of the New World with

CONNECT

Or discover great websites and books like this one at **www.facthound.com**. Just type in the book **ID: 9781496534811** and you're ready to go.